The Lost Door

The Lost Door

Dorothy Quick

ÆGYPAN PRESS

Special thanks to Greg Weeks, Mary Meehan, and the Online
Distributed Proofreading Team (which can be found at
http://www.pgdp.net).

This text from *Weird Tales,* October, 1936.

The Lost Door
A publication of
ÆGYPAN PRESS

www.aegypan.com

An alluring but deadly horror out of past centuries menaced the life of the young American — a fascinating tale of a strange and eery love.

I have often wondered whether I would have urged Wrexler to come with me if I had known what Rougemont would do to him. I think — looking back — that even if I could have glimpsed the future, I would have acted in the same way, and that I would have brought him to Rougemont to fulfill his destiny.

As the boat cut its swift way through the waters on its journey to France, I had no thought of this. Nor had Wrexler. He was happier than I had ever seen him. He had never been abroad before, and the boat was a source of wonder and enjoyment to him.

I myself was full of an eager anticipation of happy months to come. It hardly seemed possible that only a week had elapsed since I received the cable that had made such a change in my fortunes:

> Your father died yesterday. You are sole heir, provided you comply with conditions of his will, the principal one being that you spend six months of each year at Rougemont. If satisfactory, come at once.

It was signed by my father's lawyer.

I had no sorrow over my father's passing, except a deep regret that we could not have known the true relationship of father and son. At the death of my mother, my father had grown bitter and refused to see the innocent cause of her untimely passing. As a baby I had been brought up in the lodge of Rougemont, my father's magnificent château near Vichy. When I reached the age of four, I had been sent away to boarding-school. After that, my life had been a succession of schools; first in France, the adopted land of my father, then England, and finally St. Paul's in America.

In all justice to my parent, I must admit he gave me every advantage except the affection I would have cherished. By his own wish, I had never seen him in life; nor would I see him in death, for a later cable advised me that the funeral was over and his body already at rest in the beautiful Gothic mausoleum he had had built in his lifetime, after the manner of the ancients.

He had left me everything with only two injunctions, that a certain sum of money be set aside to keep the château always in its present condition and that I should spend at least half my time in it, and my children after me — a condition I was only too pleased to accept. All my life I had longed for a home.

I cabled at once that I would sail. A return cable brought me the news that I had unlimited funds to draw upon. It was then that I urged Wrexler to come with me.

*W*rexler and I had been friends since the day when two lonely boys had been put by chance into the same room at school. We were so utterly unlike, it was perhaps the difference between us that held us together through the years. At St. Paul's, and later at Princeton, Gordon Wrexler had always been at the head of his class, whereas I inevitably tagged along at the bottom. The contrast between us was expressed not only in the color of our hair and eyes, but also in our dispositions. My greatest gift from fate was a sense of humor, and I suppose it was this quality of mine that particularly appealed to Wrexler. It seems as though I was the only one who could lift him out of the despondency into which he often plunged. As the years passed, and his tendency to depression intensified, he came to depend more and more upon me, and we grew closer together.

Strangely enough, the whiteness of his face and the gloom that exuded from him did not detract from his good looks. It only added to them. For the translucence of his skin made the thick, black hair that lay close to his head all the darker, while at the same time it brought out the deep black of his eyes, and the firm cut of his lips.

The night before we landed, we were standing on deck, at the rail, looking over the side straining our eyes for the first glimpse of the lights of Cherbourg, and Wrexler spoke of himself for the first time since we had left New York.

"You know, Jim, for perhaps the only time in my life I feel at peace, as though something that I should have done long ago has been at last accomplished."

He was so solemn that I laughed a little. He stopped me suddenly: "It's true — I've always felt an urge within me, a blinding force pushing me toward something that is waiting for me: where, I do not know; what, I have no idea. For the first time, it's gone — that nameless urge that I knew not how to satisfy, and I feel that the call's being answered."

With the usual inanity of people at a loss for words, I said the first thing that came into my mind: "Perhaps Rougemont has been calling you."

"You've no idea what a relief it is," he continued, "not to feel constantly pulled with no way of knowing toward what, or how to go about answering the summons. I have often thought that I should take my life — that that was what was meant —" His voice trailed off.

This time I was not at a loss for words. I started to read him a lecture that would have done credit to Martin Luther or John Knox. At the end of my harangue Wrexler laughed, a rare thing for him, and put his arm through mine.

"All that's gone now. Didn't I tell you that at last in some strange way I am at peace?"

*R*ougemont's towers were visible long before we reached the great iron gates that had to be swung open to let us pass. For miles the great edifice dominated the landscape. The huge building had a soft, reddish tinge, from which I supposed it derived its name — Red Mountain. It was a fairy-tale palace perched on a mountain top. A great thrill went through me as I realized that this beautiful château was mine, and as we drove through the gates, up the winding road, through my own forest, the pride of possession swelled up in me and for the first time I began to understand why my father had never put his foot outside the great gates and the high wall that enclosed the acres that now belonged to me.

As we drove on, up the winding, narrow road, over the drawbridge that spanned the moat, into the courtyard, I understood more and more. Here was everything: beauty such as I had never dreamed, forests stocked with game, running brooks full of fish, a lake, and farther off, a farm — I could glimpse its thatched roofs — to supply our wants. Rougemont was a world in itself.

The high carved door was swung open as Wrexler and I got out of the car. Monsieur de Carrier, my father's lawyer, advanced to meet us, a friendly smile on his Santa Claus countenance. I shook hands, introduced Wrexler as "a very good friend who is going to stay with me."

Monsieur Carrier's face fell. Clearly Wrexler's being with me was a disappointment. Nevertheless, he greeted him politely, as he ushered us in.

That moment Rougemont took me to its heart and won me for its own.

Imagine Amboise, or any of the great French châteaux, suddenly restored to itself as it was in the days of the Medici, and you have a small idea of Rougemont. For we had stepped out of the present into the past. Carrier, Wrexler and I were anachronisms; everything else was in keeping with the dead centuries. Even the servants were in doublet and hose of a sort of cerulean blue, with great slashes puffed with crimson silk.

I think I gasped. At any rate, Monsieur Carrier saw my astonishment. "It is your father's will, my boy. He always kept it so, and wore the costume of former days, himself. He greatly admired the first Francis. In your rooms you will find costumes prepared for you. For the last six months of his life, he was making ready for his son." There was an odd sort of pride in Carrier's voice.

I remembered now that my father had written for my measurements. I had thought he meant to make me a present, but when time passed and I heard nothing, the incident had slipped from my mind. I looked at Wrexler, expecting to see some sign of amusement on his face, but he stood quietly looking at the tapestry that hung halfway up the grand stairway. There was a dreamy, faraway expression in his eyes.

"May I speak before your friend?" Carrier asked.

I nodded. The servants had already disappeared with our luggage. I threw myself down on a long, low bench, and Carrier sat opposite me.

"You understood the terms of your father's will, of course," Carrier began, "that you must live here six months, but you did not know that you must live here, as he did, in the past. If you do not, then Rougemont goes to your father's steward, with the same conditions — to be kept always as it is; with only a small sum set aside for you."

I said nothing. Driving along the road from Paris, it would have seemed fantastic, but here — under the spell of Rougemont — it seemed as though anything else would be impossible.

Carrier went on, "You will be Grand Seigneur — Lord of the Manor, in the old style. You may have your guests if you like, but they too must conform with the rules." Here he glanced at Wrexler, who still stood as though he were in a trance. "The other six months you are free to do as you please, spend what you like of the money not needed for Rougemont — that is, *if you want to go anywhere else.*"

Evidently he had finished his speech. At the time I did not recognize the significance of his last words. "I am willing to submit to the conditions; only" — a sudden thought struck me — "I don't want to lose all touch with the outside world. Can I go to Vichy — to get papers and so forth? I don't suppose they had papers in Francis First's time."

Monsieur de Carrier smiled. "My dear boy, your father didn't wish to make a prisoner of you. You may go to Vichy if you like. But you must not be away from Rougemont more than twenty-four consecutive hours during the six months you are in residence.

"So far as the papers, etc., are concerned, they will be at the lodge. There is also a telephone, and your own clothes will be kept there. After tonight, nothing of 1935 must come within these halls, but you are free to go to the lodge anytime you want to. You can get in touch with me also, if you desire further information. De Lacy, the steward, will look out for you. He knows your father's ways. Now permit me to congratulate you and say *au revoir,* my young friend."

Monsieur de Carrier got up on his stubby fat legs, made a little bow to me, another to Wrexler which went unheeded.

I too arose. "It will seem strange, but I'll do my best."

"One other thing," Monsieur de Carrier was all of a sudden very grave. "In two weeks' time you will be given a key. It unlocks a casket you will find in the library. In it you will find a message from your father. Adieu, my boy, I wish you well."

With a click of the heels and a friendly smile, he was gone.

I turned to Wrexler. "What do you think of it?" I asked.

Wrexler did not answer. He still stood gazing up at the stairway. The wide, marble steps curved upward. Along the sides, the intricate carving was beautiful in its lacy delicateness.

At that moment, however, I was alarmed for my friend. His attitude was rigid, and his eyes were glassy. I put my hand on his shoulder. "Wrexler!"

My action galvanized him to life. "Another minute and she would have reached the last step! Now she is gone."

This was madness! There had been no one there. I said as much.

Wrexler turned and faced me. "But there was," he said eagerly, "the most beautiful girl I have ever seen, all done up in some old costume: great, wide skirts, little waist, and a high lace collar. She had bronze curls, great blue eyes and the loveliest face! I saw her immediately we came in. She looked at both of us, but she smiled at me!"

I was in a quandary. Until now I had not given the staircase more than a perfunctory glance. For all I knew, she might have been one of the servants, peeping to see her new master. To Wrexler, impressionable, strange creature that he was, the one glance might have so registered on his mind that he kept on seeing her; for certainly she had not been there when I looked. It seemed best to make light of the whole matter.

"Anyway, she's gone now. At least I can explain the costume. I take it you didn't hear Carrier's announcements?"

Wrexler shook his head. I proceeded to enlighten him.

Instead of teasing me about the strange conditions my father's will had imposed upon me, he was enthusiastic about the idea. "It's the one period in history that has always interested me! Jim, we're in luck! Imagine stepping back into Medici France for six months, shutting out the world! Who knows but that Catherine herself may have stayed here, or Marguerite de Valois — the Marguerite of Marguerites! Beautiful, but no more beautiful than that girl on the stairs. I can hardly wait to see her again."

I heartily hoped that he would see her, and that she was not entirely a creature of his imagination. If she was real, I too was eager to meet her.

Wrexler interrupted my thoughts.

"I feel as though I had come home," he said. "I'm crazy to explore. Let's go shed these ugly things and begin to really live. Why, it's been this I've been waiting for! It's lucky we're the same size."

Out of his irrelevance, I gathered the trend of his thought. "I wonder where we go," I began.

Almost as though he had heard my words, a tall, commanding figure stepped into the hall. He was attired richly in damask of a lovely, soft blue with the same slashes of crimson that the servant livery had shown, but in this case of finer material. He was a handsome man of about thirty-four. His beard was pointed and he had a small mustache. His long legs were encased in silken hose and he wore a dagger thrust through his belt.

"De Lacy, at your service, my lord," he announced as he made a deep bow.

I extended my hand, somewhat at a loss to know how to greet my father's steward, who was clearly a man of some importance and who, but for me, would be owner of Rougemont.

Instead of shaking hands, he dropped on one knee and kissed my hand — a proceeding which embarrassed me very much.

On my motioning him to rise, he did so with a lithe grace: "I suppose you want to change your strange clothes, my lord, and see your quarters?"

I nodded and introduced Wrexler. De Lacy bowed. "Monsieur Wrexler would like to be near you?" Then he added, "We have some twenty or thirty suites, my lord."

Wrexler said he would prefer to be close at hand, and together we followed de Lacy up the marble stairway into a new world.

Wrexler was at ease immediately in his doublet and hose. The rich, embroidered garments seemed to suit him as modern clothes never did. He looked hand-somer than ever. He also told me that the costume of the Medici was becoming to me, and truly when I caught a glimpse of myself mirrored in the pond — for the château did not possess a large mirror — I was not ill pleased with the result. But, by the end of the week, I still felt strange in my new attire, whereas Wrexler from the beginning wore his as if to the manor born.

But I anticipate. That first night we donned two of the outfits which the valet whom de Lacy introduced to me had put out. Our own clothes disappeared, and much to my annoyance, with them my cigarettes.

*W*e ate dinner in state, upon a raised daïs at one end of a great hall. At either side below us were long, narrow tables filled with people. Dressed also in keeping with the period, they made a wonderful picture and comprised, I supposed, my court or retinue. De Lacy presented me to them with a flourish, and they all filed by and kissed my hand, then went to their places.

When Wrexler and I were seated, they too sat down. When I began to talk, they filled the hall with gay chattering. From a minstrel gallery at the other end of the room came soft strains of music.

De Lacy stood behind me pouring my wine. One thing I noticed was that in the whole room — and there must have been two hundred people at least — there were no older men or women. In fact, de Lacy was the oldest of the lot; the others ranged from about sixteen to thirty.

"How did my father get all these people together?" I asked de Lacy.

"Most of them, my lord, were born at Rougemont. Still others were adopted and brought here almost as soon as they were born. None of us has ever been outside Rougemont gates." De Lacy was quite matter-of-fact as he made his statement.

Wrexler was searching the hall with his eyes, as he listened to my steward.

"And you?" I looked at de Lacy.

"I, too, my lord, know nothing of your outside world, nor do I want to. Why should I, who am happy here? My family live down at the farm, but his Highness, your father, became interested in me. He brought me into the château, had me educated, and looked after me, himself. Eventually he made me steward of Rougemont. It is a great honor he conferred upon me and I shall do my best to help you, my lord."

Of a sudden I saw what my father's life-work had been: to rear a court to people Rougemont. My father had been twenty-five at my mother's death. He had died at fifty-eight. He had had thirty-three years to make his dream come true.

"Where are the parents of the ones who were born at Rougemont?"

"At their own places, or the farms, my lord. Rougemont has over a thousand acres and several manors upon it, where people whom his Highness your father advanced over others, live. They all serve their ruler in some way, in return for what is given them. Only the people of the lodge are in touch with the Outside, which we have been taught to look upon with scorn. Here we have everything, and to be taken to the château itself is the ambition of everyone on the estate."

I saw it all; not, of course, every intricacy of the elaborate system my father had evolved, but at least a glimmer of the truth. And I marveled at the character of a man who had taken children out of the world to make his own world and then had the patience to wait for them to grow up; to form his court — the court he planned for me. Yes, in my egotism I thought it was for me! Two weeks were to pass before I learned what his real reason had been.

Into my reflections, Wrexler broke abruptly, "She is not here. Ask de Lacy about her; her beauty haunts me. Already I am in love with her."

I was not surprized. Nothing, I felt, could at this point surprize me, so much had happened in the last few hours. If my father had arisen from the floor like Hamlet's ghost, I would have greeted him quite casually.

"Is there a young girl here with bronze curls and blue eyes?" I asked obediently.

A shadow crossed de Lacy's handsome face. For the first time he hesitated. "There is no one here that answers that description. May I ask why you —"

"My friend saw her on the stairway."

I caught a murmur from de Lacy's lips, "So soon!" it sounded like, but before I could question further, he said aloud, "I have leave to depart and join my lady?" And before I could answer, he bowed himself away to take a seat at one of the tables below.

Wrexler looked over his wine goblet. "The man lied. I saw recognition of the description in his eyes."

"We'll get the truth out of him later," I countered. "Isn't it fine to actually eat chicken with your fingers, and not feel you are committing a social error!"

*W*e did not get any information out of de Lacy later. To Wrexler's insistent questionings he was at first non-committal, and after a bit, downright curt. I poured oil on the troubled waters by suggesting that as it was late, we would wait until morning to see the library and the left wing of the château.

With a smile of relief, de Lacy ushered us to our chambers. My retiring was a kind of ceremony. It amused me, but I had a nagging little thought in the back of my mind that all this etiquette would become boring after a while.

As the last man bowed himself out of my room, de Lacy bent low. "My lord, there are guards at your door. You have only to call if you require anything."

I thanked him once more. Greatly to my embarrassment, he again kissed my hand. "Your servant to the death!" he cried, and drew the curtains about my high-canopied bed.

I knew that outside the red damask, two huge candles were burning, but the curtain shut out their light and I was smothered in darkness. I made a mental note that I must arrange somehow for air in my room. The French idea of banishing night air did not coincide with my American habits. Tonight I was too weary to get up and attend to it. My thoughts were racing back and forth among the strange events of the day, but before I could focus them into any kind of order, sleep descended upon me.

I had a strange dream. In it, the most beautiful woman I had ever seen came and parted the red damask curtains. Framed against the dark oak panels of my room, she stood looking down upon me. Her hair was red gold, and her eyes had all the sapphire tints of the world stored in their depths. Her pale, white face was oval in shape and balanced perfectly upon a slender neck. Her lips were sweetly curved and her nose delicately shaped. As she bent over me, I could see the rounded curve of her bosom. One slim hand reached out and touched my cheek. It was like the touch of a falling rose petal.

In my dream I lay asleep, yet I was conscious of this lovely creature. I watched her through closed eyelids, and held my breath, hoping she would kiss me. It seemed as though I had never desired anything so much.

A half-smile hovered on her lips, but her eyes told me nothing. She leaned lower. A faint perfume pervaded my senses, and then I felt her lips upon my forehead. A great cold swept over me at her touch — swept me down, down into blackness, and I knew no more.

*W*hen I awoke, the sun was pouring through the opened curtains. I reached for a cigarette — my first conscious thought upon awakening — and not finding my case under the pillow, suddenly realized my new surroundings. At the same time, I remembered my dream. "Wrexler and his talk of a red-haired beauty is responsible for that," I thought as I clapped my hands.

De Lacy came in so quickly I knew he must have been waiting outside the door. He started when he saw the curtain of my bed had been opened. "Did you not pull them?" I asked.

He shook his head. I said no more, and the ceremony of my arising began.

When I had bathed in a great sunken tub — fortunately Diana de Poictiers had had her daily bath in the far-off time — I sought Wrexler.

Together we breakfasted, and then I announced to de Lacy that we wished to inspect the rest of the château. He led us to the left wing, and took us through suite after suite. Beautifully furnished, the château was a veritable treasure house. An antiquarian would have gone mad with delight.

I noticed that de Lacy had avoided two heavily built doors opposite the ballroom. When we had returned from our tour, I stopped before them. "And here?" I asked.

"The picture gallery, my lord," he responded unwillingly, and swung the doors open. There was an unhappy expression on his face.

The room was long and narrow, and the walls except for the windows were lined with portraits. We walked slowly down the length of the room, looking at the portraits of a dead and gone race.

"The former owners of the château?" I asked. De Lacy nodded.

Suddenly I looked at the part of the room facing the door which he had entered. At first we had been too far away to distinguish anything about it except that there was only one large painting hanging in the center. Now that I was nearer, I could see the painting, and I caught my breath in astonishment; for there was the portrait of the lady of my dream, smiling down on me.

Wrexler caught my arm, "That's the girl — the one I saw on the stairs."

"That is the portrait of Hélène, Mademoiselle d'Harcourt, daughter of the Lord of Harcourt, who owned this château," de Lacy's voice broke in.

Wrexler and I exclaimed simultaneously, "But I —" and "She is —"

De Lacy looked at us strangely. "It is from her that the château got its new name Rougemont — *Red Mountain*. Before that, it was called Hôtel d'Harcourt. Mademoiselle Hélène was very beautiful, as you can see, *Messieurs,* and she had many suitors. At last, from among them, she chose an English lord. One of the discarded lovers, Black George — *le Georges Noir* — vowed that she should not belong to the Englishman, or ever leave Rougemont.

"She laughed, Mademoiselle Hélène, and her father, the Lord d'Harcourt, laughed too, for he had many men at arms and was rich and powerful. Black George did not laugh, he only set his lips grimly. The wedding day came and the beautiful Hélène married the English lord in the great hall, but just as he took her in his arms for the nuptial kiss, there arose a great noise outside. It was Black George attacking the château.

"The English lord, with Hélène's kiss warm upon his lips, went forth to battle. There was a fight such as these peaceful lands had never seen, and the mountain ran red with blood. Black George was the victor. He slew the Englishman, he slew the Lord of Harcourt, and his men hacked to pieces the defenders of the château.

"Black George, followed by his men, their swords red with blood, came into the great hall where Hélène d'Harcourt sat on the throne, her face whiter than her wedding dress. Black George flung her lover's body at her feet, and the women of the household who were crouched about the throne cried aloud with terror. The fair Hélène did not cry, nor did she moan; she only looked straight at Black George, and there was that in her gaze that silenced everyone in the great hall; even Black George stepped back a pace.

"Then Hélène d'Harcourt rose and went down to her love, the English lord who for a brief moment had been her husband. She knelt beside him and kissed his cold lips; then she took her wedding veil and laid it over his body.

"All the while there was silence in the great hall, while men and women watched the slim girl say farewell to the man she loved. They watched almost as though they were under a spell. But as the veil fell into place, Black George laughed a long laugh that rang through the room; then he turned to his followers, and cried loudly, 'The women are yours — take them as you will, all but that one who belongs to me.' He gestured toward Hélène and laughed again.

"Hélène d'Harcourt stood erect and pointed her slender hand at Black George. 'Wait,' she cried, and there was a quality in her voice that made her listeners tremble. 'I shall belong to no one until my lover comes for me, and till he comes, wo to you, Black George, who are well named! Wo to you and to all men, for I curse you with a mighty curse, the curse of a broken heart. And I curse all men for their black and bitter deeds. Year after year, century after century, I will take my vengeance for the wrongs I have suffered, and no man shall be free until my lover comes again and we find bliss together.'

"And while the eyes of the whole hall were riveted upon her, she plunged the dagger she had taken from her lover's belt into her heart. For a second she stood swaying; then she crumpled and fell beside the English lord.

"Black George caught her and held her in his arms. 'My curse upon you, Black George!' she cried.

"Black George could also curse — 'Never shall you leave Rougemont to find your lover, and never shall he come, until —' and then his voice died away as her head fell backward over his arm. The fair Hélène was beyond his reach.

"For a minute more the people in the great hall were paralyzed by the force of the terrible words that they had heard, but with the girl's death they were released from the spell and a fury swept over the men. They rushed upon the women and dragged them forth. Black George took Hélène's body and carried it away, but where he buried her no one knew, nor could any discover; for the next day he was found in the great hall raving mad, and the people said that Hélène's curse was a potent one, that already it had wreaked vengeance on the one who had wronged her most.

"From that day, the château was called Rougemont. The d'Harcourts were all dead and the place fell into other hands. Then there grew up the rumor that the château was haunted, that the fair Hélène roamed through its halls, cut off from her lover, and doomed to stay within these walls by Black George's curse."

*D*e Lacy silent, Wrexler and I looked at the portrait. My own feelings were in a turmoil. It had been a ghost's lips that had touched me last night; yet surely no ghosts could have been so beautiful or seemed so real.

Wrexler turned to me, "It would be the curse that has always been upon me that when I fell in love it would be with a ghost!" His eyes were vivid, shining brightly in his pale face. "I knew when I saw her on the stairway that I loved her."

"There is a rumor," said de Lacy, "that the man who sees the fair Hélène will meet with some misadventure, unless she gives him a kiss. Then he is protected from her wrath."

I started. Wrexler smiled. "She kissed me with her eyes. I am not afraid."

"The fair Hélène makes men suffer to make up for the wrong Black George did her. For years she has not been seen at Rougemont. Last night when you described her, I was afraid. My lord," de Lacy turned to me, "send your friend away. If she only looked at him and smiled, there is a grave and deadly danger for him, more deadly because it may be unexplainable. Men upon whom the fair Hélène has smiled have met strange deaths."

As Wrexler looked up at the portrait, an inward light illumined his countenance. "I am not afraid," he repeated.

"There are many deaths. There is the death of the spirit as well as that of the body. I beg you to go while there is time, friend of my lord." There was real feeling in de Lacy's voice.

I too felt afraid for Wrexler. The strange, unworldly feeling he had always had, the pulling toward something he knew not what, made me doubly fearful. Had the fair Hélène been calling him all this time, across the world? For myself I had no fear. She had kissed me, and besides, even death at her hands would have been preferable to never seeing her again. In these last few minutes I had realized that I too was in love with Hélène, that I could hardly wait for the night, in hopes that she might visit me again.

Resolutely I put my own feelings in the background, for at the moment Wrexler was of paramount importance. If there was anything in de Lacy's story — and from my own experience I was sure there was — Wrexler was in danger. I turned to him. "If anything happened to you, I could never forgive myself. Perhaps you'd better go. I could arrange a trip for you, and later — meet you."

Somehow de Lacy seemed one of us. I had no hesitancy in speaking before him. He seemed a part of my new life. With the strange suddenness that comes on rare occasions, we were already friends.

Wrexler looked at me, then back at the portrait. Hélène d'Harcourt, her red hair gleaming, smiled down upon us. Before he spoke, I knew what he would say, because in his place I would have said the same, "Unless you kick me out, I want to stay."

I put my hand on Wrexler's shoulder. "So be it. Come along, let's see the library, then we'll know all of Rougemont. We've seen everything else."

Wrenching his eyes away from the portrait, Wrexler followed us.

The library was beautiful, with paneled walls that had rows and rows of books sunk in their depths. There was a long, oaken table, and on the center of it stood a carved, gilded box, the casket which held my father's letter. I wished then that I could read it at once. I wish now that I could have, but perhaps it is better that I did not; at least things moved as the fates ordained, and the responsibility for what occurred was not mine.

*T*he next three days were quiet, happy ones. Nothing occurred. I had no ghostly visitant and Wrexler saw nothing of Hélène. Under de Lacy's expert guidance, we rode over the estate, hunted with falcons, a pleasing sport which we both took to our hearts; mingled with my court, found the people charming and highly cultivated. We took lessons in the old dances, visited the manor houses. It was all very gay and amusing, and I had no longing for the outside world. I did not even go down to the lodge for news.

There were many details of the estate management that I had to go into with de Lacy. We spent several hours each morning going over the affairs of Rougemont. It was virtually a small kingdom, and everything was referred to me.

Necessarily, the time I spent with de Lacy on such matters, Wrexler was alone. He had changed a great deal since we had come to Rougemont. He had come alive, and he threw himself into everything with a curious intensity. He was like a person who has been very ill, who suddenly finding himself better and fearing it is only temporary, clutches life with both hands. He devoted long hours to reading the records of the d'Harcourts, until he knew the family history as well as his own.

I did not mention Hélène, although there was seldom a moment when she was out of my thoughts. I found myself watching for her day and night, and I caught the same tension in Wrexler's eyes as he searched the shadows.

The third night she came again, not to me, but to Wrexler; and although he was my friend, I almost hated him because he had seen her and I had not. He told me next morning as we walked along the lake shore.

"Jim," he said suddenly, "I saw her last night. She came to my room. She drew aside the curtains of the bed, and leaned over me. I can't describe my sensations. It was almost as though life were suspended in space — like a bridge over a timeless sea."

I had nothing to say. I knew so well how he felt.

"She leaned closer and closer to me," Wrexler went on; "then she smiled, and before I could find my breath to speak, she was gone. This is the second time she has smiled at me. I felt a nameless fear, as though there was a threatening quality in those red lips. She looked at me as though I might have been Black George himself."

In that moment, all my envy was swept away by anxiety for my friend. Indeed, I wished she had kissed him, for then he would have been safe. I started to speak, to beg Wrexler to leave Rougemont, but before the words could leave my mouth, I saw her. She was standing in the path some distance away, directly in line with my eyes, and she was shaking her head impressively.

I knew instantly what she meant. I was not to send Wrexler away. He could not see her, because at the moment he was facing me, his hand on my arm. His fingers touching me were not quite steady. It brought me back to reality. "Wrexler," I cried, "you — could leave Rougemont."

Her eyes clouded with anger. She looked at me reproachfully, commandingly. As though I were dreaming, I heard my own voice, "I don't want you to go, I would be lonely without you. Perhaps there is no danger."

Wrexler looked at me curiously. "There is risk, I know that, but I do not care, I am like a man who has eaten a strange and terrible drug, who knows the danger, but can not resist it. I will stay."

Beyond him Hélène smiled a satisfied smile, as she looked at Wrexler's broad back. It made me feel afraid. Then suddenly her gaze swept to me, and the smile changed into a languorous one that promised all things. My heart beat faster, and I forgot my fear.

Wrexler moved restlessly, turning so that we were side by side. Even in that second Hélène had vanished — how, I do not know. One minute she was there, the next she was not.

We walked along slowly. Finally Wrexler spoke. "No matter what happens, and I mean that widely, my friend, you are not to regret. For a little time I have been happy. I have come alive. I have loved, even though the woman that I love is a wraith. I have felt a sensation I thought never to feel. If I could hold her in my arms and press my lips to hers, I would count the world well lost."

I could say nothing, because — God pity me! — I knew just how he felt.

*T*he days slipped away quickly. I did not see Hélène again, but Wrexler did. Almost every day he met her in the rose garden, where they spent long hours.

He told me that she was always elusive, but at the same time promising that some day she would be kinder. He said her voice was like golden honey and that without her he could not face life.

Once I saw them myself, as I came from an interview with de Lacy. As I approached the rose garden through an opening in the arches, I saw them sitting side by side on the marble bench, and of the two, Hélène looked the more earthly. For Wrexler had grown paler and more ethereal every day. His eyes were luminous as he looked at her adoringly.

She saw me first, and her lips curved sweetly. She rose in a leisurely fashion, turned her back to me and dropped a low curtsy to Wrexler; then while I still watched, she extended one slender hand to him. He bent over it, his lips touched its soft whiteness. A little laugh like the tinkle of silver bells swept through the garden; then she was gone.

Wrexler stood like a man in a trance. I came quickly forward. "You are playing with fire!" I cried.

Wrexler roused. "You saw?"

I nodded.

"Have you ever seen anything more beautiful, more lovely?"

I shook my head.

"I'm not afraid anymore. She has promised me —"

But what Hélène had promised I was not to know, for Wrexler's mouth shut with a snap. When I pressed him, he shook his head. Finally he said, carefully choosing his words with a reluctance that was strange to him:

"To me is to be granted something beyond the knowledge of mortal man. I can tell you no more, but some day you will know." There was an expression on his face that transcended earth.

The next night I spoke to de Lacy and told him my fears. Wrexler was spending more and more time in the rose garden. I hardly saw him, and he would not discuss anything with me. Even at the stately, elegantly served meals, he barely spoke. He always seemed to be listening, waiting.

De Lacy shared my fears, but he suggested nothing to help. "He has been marked, my lord," he said gravely. "We can only pray. But even in prayers there is no refuge, for Hélène is beyond such things."

"Surely —" I began to remonstrate.

"The power of evil is as strong as the power of good, or at least there is little between them. Hélène herself is bound fast by hate of Black George."

Curses live, I knew that — witness the lasting quality of the curses and spells of the Egyptian priests. But Hélène was not evil. I said as much.

De Lacy shook his head. "She is cut off from her lover. She does not feel kindly toward men. Remember she promised vengeance century after century, that day in the great hall."

That night in the silence of my chamber I called her name. "Hélène! Hélène!" I flung my agonized summons into the night, but there was no answer.

I went over in my mind the tales de Lacy had told me of the havoc she had caused; how one man had cast himself down from the highest turret, crying her name; how another had been found dead in the rose garden, horror frozen on his face. There were still others who had looked upon her, and death or madness came as the result.

The more I thought of these tales of terror, the more I feared for Wrexler. At last I could stand no more. I thrust my arms into the rich velvet robe that had taken the place of my bath gown, and went to Wrexler's room. The guards stood back to let me pass.

I did not mean to wake him, but some inner foreboding made me feel I must know that he was safe.

As I drew aside the curtains of his bed, I could not entirely stifle the cry that came to my lips, for the bed was empty. But upon the pillow lay a small, white rose. It was the kind they use in funeral wreaths in France. My heart almost stopped beating.

The rose garden! — or perhaps the library. A more normal thought struck me. Wrexler might have wanted to read. I rushed into the hall, to find de Lacy waiting for me, summoned by the guards. He held a silver candlestick in which a tall, white candle burned.

"The library!" I gasped. That was nearest, we should try it first. De Lacy knew my meaning. He had instantly grasped the situation and his face was white and tense.

Together we descended the curving stairway. Together we reached the library. Then, motioning de Lacy behind me, I swung open the door.

The room was brightly illuminated, although not one of the candles had been lit. In the middle of it stood Wrexler, with Hélène in his arms. Their lips were close-locked.

It was a picture that an artist would have delighted to paint: the stiff, crimson skirts of Hélène d'Harcourt's gown stood wide on either side, and Wrexler's blue doublet and hose against them was in bold relief. His long oversleeves edged with fur hung gracefully.

I could not speak. This mating of man with ghost was almost more than my poor mortal brain could bear, yet with every atom of my being I wished that I could have been in Wrexler's place. I remembered the one chaste kiss I had had from her, and I almost fainted at the thought of possessing those lips for my own, as Wrexler was doing. Strangely enough, mingling with this emotion was another — a feeling of fear and anxiety for my friend. Cold horror that froze my blood kept me rooted to the spot.

Behind me de Lacy had fallen to his knees. I could hear him repeating the Latin words of a prayer. All at once I saw where the light was coming from. The entire north wall, ordinarily lined with books, had gone. In its stead was a stone wall, and in the center of the wall was a low-hung Gothic door, carved and ornate. It was standing open, and beyond was a pale, luminous yellow mist. I could see nothing of what else was beyond the door, for the yellow haze filled the entire space. It was like a golden fog, and its radiance lighted the library with a strange, unearthly glow. Its luminosity glowed upon Hélène and Wrexler like a spotlight.

For a moment I thought Rougemont, de Lacy, everything of the past weeks, must have been a dream and that I was watching a cinema of past days. All at once, before my astonished eyes Hélène gently drew her lips away from Wrexler's. She slipped from his arms and extended her hands to him. "Come," I heard her say.

Wrexler had been right: her voice was like golden honey. It was like the music of willow trees in early spring. Wrexler grasped her hands. For the first time I saw his face. Joy transfigured it, such joy as I have never seen before, and never shall see again.

Hélène moved backward, slowly but surely, drawing him toward the little Gothic door that stood open. With her soft lips half parted, she whispered, "Come."

"Wrexler," I cried suddenly.

He did not hear me. As he looked into her eyes, he might have been a bird charmed by a snake. Nothing could break through the spell that bound him.

They were nearer the door. Each second brought them closer to it. Now Hélène was on the other side. The golden mist concentrated upon her, until she looked like a goddess in its eery light.

"Wrexler! Wrexler!" The words tore through my throat.

Wrexler stepped over the threshold. Through the golden mist I saw him clasp Hélène in his arms again. I saw her smile triumphantly at me, as she raised her lips to his. There was something in her eyes that filled me with horror.

The mist swirled about them until I could barely discover the outlines of their figures through its gleaming haze. Then the door swung slowly shut.

I awoke to feverish activity. "Wrexler! Wrexler!" I shouted and rushed forward to the door.

I grasped the iron ring that hung in its center. I pulled on it with all my might. When I found that it resisted all my efforts I began beating against the door itself. Presently I felt myself being pulled away.

"There is no use, my lord," de Lacy's voice was saying. "The door is gone."

"Gone!" I ejaculated, and even as I spoke I saw what he meant. The north wall of the library was lined with books as it always had been. I had been beating upon them impotently.

I looked down at my hands; the knuckles were raw and bleeding, just as they would have been from pounding on a heavily carved wooden door. De Lacy caught my meaning. "The door was there, my lord. It was the lost door — the door behind which Black

George buried Hélène d'Harcourt. It had been lost for centuries."

I sank into a chair, weakly, for now the fact that I had lost Wrexler, my friend, was paramount. "I will tear down the walls until I find it."

"That has been done, my lord, and it has never been found. It will never be found again. Only for a brief moment you and I have been granted a glimpse of something we can not understand."

"And Wrexler —" I groaned.

"He was happy," de Lacy comforted. "No matter what happened after, he has had happiness such as I have never seen before."

My head pitched forward and I knew no more.

*T*hree days later, I was escorted to the library by de Lacy, to whom since Wrexler's loss I was more devoted than ever. With great ceremony I was given the key to the gilded casket, then left alone.

Seated in the great chair before the oaken table, I unlocked the casket. It contained many pages closely written in my father's hand. In them were instructions as to my future conduct, my care of Rougemont, what he had done and what he expected me to do. But the lines that interested me most were these:

"*I bought Rougemont for your mother, shortly after your birth, because when riding through this country, she saw and loved it. It was a purchase that cost me dear. For Rougemont held a curse and an avenging spirit in the form of a beautiful young girl who could not bear to see others' happiness. So my wife died.*

"*Two months after your mother's death, I first saw la belle Hélène. We fought a long battle, she and I, but I was strong, my son, because I loved your mother. No other woman's charms could lure me to my doom. Finally I made a bargain with a ghost.*

"She hated modern things and longed for Rougemont to be great again. I promised to restore the château to its former splendor, to make it just as it had been in her days, and in return she promised immunity to me, and afterward to you, and to all my court when I should have established it.

"I restored Rougemont. I repeopled it. With her help and advice, I have made it as it was in her own day.

"She showed me the hidden treasure vaults of the d'Harcourts so that I would have enough money to purchase the things she wanted.

"She too has kept her bargain, for I and my court have lived happily here unmolested. Only when an outsider came or someone disobeyed or longed for the outside world, has she wreaked vengeance.

"She has sworn to give you the kiss that promises immunity, the night you come. Only, beware, my son, whom you bring here from the world you know, and beware of the lovely Hélène. Old man as I am, devoted to your mother's memory as I am, she can still make my pulses leap.

"Above all things, if she shows you the Lost Door, do not be tempted to cross its threshold, for that way, unless you are the reincarnation of the Englishman, annihilation lies."

There was more, pages more, of other matters, but I left them for another day. Alone there in the library, I let my eyes wander to where the little Gothic door had been.

Had Wrexler been the Englishman come back to earth to claim his bride? Could that account for the strange, unsatisfied longings he had always had, his unearthly feelings, his unlikeness to other people? Or was he Black George, lured back to Rougemont for Hélène's vengeance? I hope for his sake that was not the explanation; that he and Hélène would find bliss waiting for them behind the Lost Door and I would never see Hélène again.

The days pass. I do what my father set out for me to do. I keep his bargain with the ghost of the fair Hélène. I never leave Rougemont. I have no desire to, for I am always hoping that some day I shall again find the Lost Door.

CPSIA information can be obtained
at www.ICGtesting.com
Printed in the USA
BVHW030247021218
534551BV00001B/50/P

9 781463 801373